Peter's Special Concoction

How a Little Boy Learned to Manage Type 1 Diabetes

Author: <u>Angela Cleveland</u>

Illustrator: <u>Beth Pierce</u>

Confident Counselor Publishing

ISBN: 069205460X
ISBN-13: 978-0692054604

TABLE OF CONTENTS

DEDICATION

This book is dedicated to my very special nephew who was diagnosed with Type 1 Diabetes when he was just five-years-old.

This book is also dedicated to every child who is learning to manage a lifelong disease and the families who love them, who fight a battle against an invisible enemy for them, and who hold a child's pain in their hearts in the hopes that they can carry some of the burden their little bodies bear.

ACKNOWLEDGMENTS

I would like to express my gratitude to mentors and colleagues. As a school counselor, I am blessed to work with a wonderful group of teachers and colleagues who have graciously assisted with content and editing. Our school nurse, Valerie Newman, has generously given her time and expertise to explain medical complexities to me. Her assistance is much appreciated!

I am continually thankful for the many supportive people in my life who cheer me on and encourage me to follow my dreams - my husband and number one editor, Scott Cleveland, persuaded me to formally publish; and my aunt, Cheri Montgomery, who has relentlessly encouraged and persistently pushed me to "write an article, a book, write something!" I am glad that I finally listened, and I am grateful that she continues to motivate me to write stories that help children and families.

CHAPTER 1:

SOMETHING IS WRONG

"Daddy, Peter looks sick," Mommy said with a worried frown. Peter sat on a gleaming silver and red stool at the counter of Cranberry Kitchens Family Restaurant. His little hands wrapped around a tall glass of water. His lips curled around a large green plastic swirly straw whose loops filled with water as Peter drank. It was the fourth time Mommy refilled his glass that afternoon.

Daddy looked at Peter. "Hmmm," he murmured as he untied his apron and walked from behind the counter to sit on a stool next to Peter.

"He has been drinking a lot of water lately," Mommy observed. "He seems so tired, too. Usually Peter can't wait to slip on the rubber gloves to make the most popular item on the menu: 'Peter's Special Salad.'" Customers from all over New Jersey flocked to Cranberry Kitchen Family Restaurant to devour Peter's delicious salad. It was the perfect combination of crunchy lettuce, crisp cucumbers, and sweet bits of fresh fruit.

Daddy pressed his hand against Peter's forehead. It felt hot against his palm. Peter finished his glass of water, and he laid his cheek against the cool, clean countertop. He tried to keep his eyes open, but he felt so tired. Mommy rubbed Peter's back as his heavy eyelids closed.

"This morning, he was really grumpy," Daddy said. "A couple of weeks ago, he couldn't wait for enough leaves to fall from the oak trees in yard so we could create a humongous, crunchy leaf pile. He wanted to leap into it with Dusty and Ranger. Today, he didn't even want to play with them. Something is definitely wrong if Peter can resist their playful, puppy licks and wagging tails."

"Yes," Mommy agreed. "And usually Peter makes up funny songs and dances to make Molly laugh while I change her diaper. Today, he just wanted to take a nap."

"He had that stomach bug last week," Daddy recalled, "but that seemed to pass." Daddy's eyes met Mommy's.

What was wrong with Peter?

"Daddy," said Mommy, "we should take Peter to the hospital." Daddy looked at Peter and slowly nodded his head.

CHAPTER 2:

THE HOSPITAL

Daddy took Peter to the hospital. It was a big building with many nurses in colorful scrubs and doctors in white coats who took care of people who didn't feel well. Peter's eyes slid around the waiting room, curious about why the other people were at the hospital.

He observed a little girl with pigtails in a bright yellow dress. Her knees had scrapes on them and her eyes looked sad. The girl cradled her right arm, which was nestled in a blue sling. Her

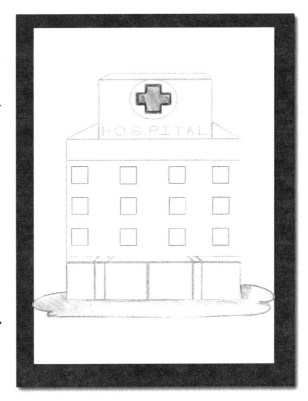

mommy sat next to her with her arm wrapped around the little girl's shoulders.

She kissed the girl on the forehead and said, "You can pick out the color of the cast, and everybody in your class can sign it." The little girl smiled up at her mommy. "And, how about we avoid climbing trees until you are all better?"

The little girl nodded. "Okay," she agreed. Peter thought about the big oak trees in his yard. There was one tree he loved to climb. Mommy and Daddy told him where he was allowed to climb up to and no higher. They painted a red line on the bark of the tree to mark the spot so he would not forget. He could understand why the little girl loved to climb trees since it was one of his favorite things to do.

A nurse with a clipboard walked into the waiting room. "Peter?" he called out. Daddy raised his hand and waved to the nurse. Then, he scooped up Peter in his arms, and followed the nurse as he led them to a room in the hospital. In the center of the room, there was a bed on wheels in it in. A counter with jars of wooden sticks, cotton balls, and bandages lined one side of the room. A blinking screen on a pole stood between two chairs on the other side of the room.

Peter immediately noticed the most interesting thing in the room: a small black-cushioned little stool on wheels. It looked kid-sized! He imagined placing his belly on the cushion, getting a running start, and then lifting his legs to fly across the hospital. He could almost hear the flap of his superhero cape behind him and feel the wind in his hair. "Weeee..." he whispered to himself. If he wasn't so tired, he would ask Daddy to let him try it.

"I'm Nurse Scott," the man introduced himself as Daddy lowered Peter into the bed. Nurse Scott arranged pillows around Peter's head. "The doctors and I are curious about what is happening inside Peter's body." Daddy scooted a chair next to the bed and held Peter's hand.

Nurse Scott held up a metal tool with a plastic tip that was attached by a wire to the blinking screen on the pole.

"This is a thermometer (ther-**mom**-ma-ter). It tells us the temperature inside your body when you hold it under your tongue." Peter nodded. Mommy and Daddy had taken his temperature just last week when he was sick with the stomach bug.

"Ahhhh!" Peter said as he opened his mouth wide. Nurse Scott smiled and placed the thermometer in Peter's mouth. Nurse Scott looked at the screen. It beeped and flashed the number "100." He removed the thermometer from Peter's mouth and set it aside.

Nurse Scott picked up another tool with a tiny bright light at the tip. "This is called an otoscope (**oh**-toe-scope). It's a tiny flashlight, and it helps me to see inside your ears. Is it okay if I look inside your ears," Nurse Scott asked. Peter nodded.

Nurse Scott leaned over and shined the light in Peter's right ear and then his left ear. "Hmmm," he said. "I think I know the problem." Nurse Scott stood up and shook his head with a tiny smile forming at the corners of his mouth.

Peter's eyes widened, "You do?"

"I think so. Have you been using your ears as a piggy bank?" Peter shook his head no. "I ask because...." Nurse Scott reached toward Peter's left ear and then moved his hand in front of Peter. A shiny silver quarter lay in Nurse Scott's hand. "...I found this in your ear."

Daddy laughed and Peter eyes got even wider. He picked up the coin and turned it over in his hand. "We will still need to learn more about what's going on inside your body, Peter," Nurse Scott said with a smile.

CHAPTER 3:

THE DOCTOR

"Is this Peter's room," asked a doctor in a blue coat holding a blue clipboard. She had light hair, almost the same yellow color as the girl's dress in the waiting room.

The doctor walked into the hospital room and extended her hand to Peter. "I'm Doctor Valerie." Peter shook her hand. He felt like a grownup!

Peter noticed a hose with a metal disc on one end and large horseshoe shape of the hose at the other end. As Doctor Valerie spoke with Daddy and Nurse Scott, Peter wondered about the hose-disc necklace. Was it a medical tool or jewelry?

Doctor Valerie finished her conversation with Daddy and Nurse Scott and turned toward Peter. "I see you noticed my stethoscope (**steth**-oh-scope)," she said as she removed it from around her neck. "It helps me to hear your heart beating and your lungs as you breathe. Do you want to try it?"

Peter nodded his head. "Yes," he whispered, filled with curiosity.

"Here," she said, handing Peter the horseshoe-end shape. "Put these metal tips in your ears." Peter slipped the cold-metal rounded ends in his ears. Doctor Valerie pressed the disc end of the stethoscope to the left side of her chest. Suddenly Peter's ears filled with a "lub-dub, lub-dub" sound.

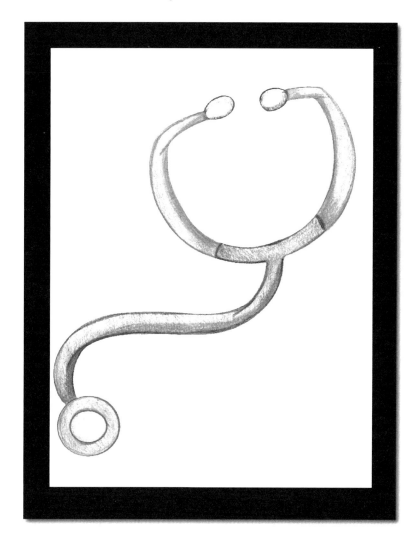

"Can you hear that?" Doctor Valerie asked. Peter nodded. "That's the sound of my heart beating. Do you want to hear what your heart sounds like?" Peter nodded. Doctor Valerie placed the metal disc on Peter's chest. Again, Peter's ears filled. "Lub-dub, lub-dub."

"Wow..." Peter whispered. He could hear his heart

beating!

"It's pretty cool," added Nurse Scott with a knowing nod. Peter nodded back.

"Can I listen?" Doctor Valerie asked. Peter nodded and handed her the horseshoe-end of the stethoscope. Doctor Valerie slipped the stethoscope into her ears and listened.

"Daddy, I could hear my own heart!" Peter exclaimed as Doctor Valerie moved the disc on his chest and on his back to listen to Peter's heart and lungs.

Daddy chuckled and squeezed Peter's hand.

"Everything sounds great," Doctor Valerie announced as she slipped the stethoscope back around her shoulders. "There's one more thing I want to do. I'd like to get a closer look at your blood, Peter. It can tell us so much helpful information about what is happening inside your body."

"How will you get my blood?" Peter whispered, fear creeping into his voice.

"We use tiny needles…" Doctor Valerie explained. Peter squeezed his Daddy's hand as hard as he could.

"Daddy, will it hurt?" Peter's eyes were wide and filled with worry.

Daddy smiled calmly at Peter and replied, "It will be a pinch, and it will only sting a little bit." Peter looked at Daddy and slowly nodded his head. He trusted his Daddy because he was wise and strong and knew a lot of things.

Peter whispered to Doctor Valerie, "Okay, I'll be brave." He took a deep breath. He could hear Nurse Scott and Doctor Valerie arranging something on the counter, but he could not see what. Their bodies blocked his view of the counter.

'Be brave,' Peter thought to himself. 'But *how?*'

Nurse Scott held up a tiny wet towel. "This is just alcohol to clean the skin on the inside of your arm." Peter nervously held out his arm to Nurse Scott who wiped down his skin. His eyes got bigger and bigger as he watched Nurse Scott clean his arm. His skin felt cool and tingled where Nurse Scott cleaned it with the alcohol.

Daddy said firmly to Peter, "Peter look at me. Look in

my eyes." Peter turned his head toward Daddy and looked into his soft brown eyes. "Peter, did you know that being in the hospital is actually...interesting? It reminds me of your scientist kit at home. You told me about how mixing two different colors can make a brand new color. That's pretty cool! What are some new things you are seeing and learning here in the hospital?"

Peter was confused. He thought, 'Why was Daddy talking about cool things right now? What did his scientist kid have to do with... wait ...Ah ha!' When Peter played "scientist," Mommy or Daddy dropped brightly colored food dye into beakers and flasks filled with water. Peter liked swirling and mixing the colors to create new colors. When he created a new color, he called it his "concoction." Only, that was a pretend concoction. The hospital was *more exciting* because it was *real!*

Peter nearly shouted in excitement, "Doctors and nurses are like scientists! They are learning what is happening in my body to help them make a special concoction to heal me!"

"That's right!" Daddy said with a big smile. "Now squeeze my hand and let's think about happy thoughts, okay?"

Peter squeezed Daddy's hand tightly. Peter squeezed his eyes shut.

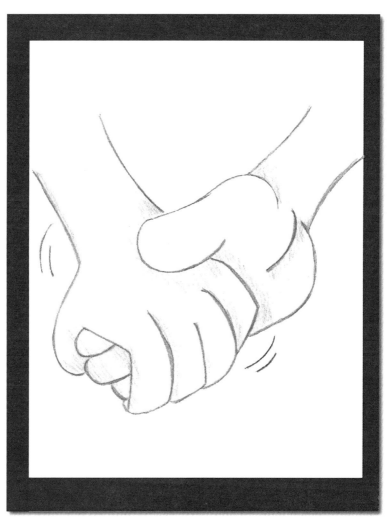

"Do you remember how you made the orange concoction?" Daddy asked.

Peter nodded. "We had to make the red and yellow first."

"Yes!" Daddy agreed. Peter recalled how the drops of food dye in the water started off very dark and brightly colored. When Peter mixed the water and dye together with his spoon, the water seemed to magically turn a lighter shade of that color. Peter's thoughts drifted to his scientist kit as Daddy continued to ask him questions, reminding him of all of the concoctions he created.

Peter let the scary thoughts flow out of his head. He kept the happy thoughts in his head.

CHAPTER 4:

FLOWING THOUGHTS

Can you really let scary thoughts flow out of your mind and hold the happy thoughts in your head?

Peter had a special trick. He thought about Cranberry Kitchens Family Restaurant, where he worked with his Mommy and Daddy. Peter thought about one of his favorite foods: spaghetti. He loved the long noodles with butter and lots of "spaghetti sprinkles" (which was really parmesan cheese).

Eating spaghetti was more than yummy; it was a fun experience! Peter loved slowly spinning his fork on his plate, capturing lots of noodles in a ball. He loved lifting the fork to his mouth and watching the noodles unwind. Slurp! Peter loved sucking in the noodles and watching them twirl before his eyes. His lips were left coated in warm butter and sprinkles of delicious cheese.

Peter imagined the spaghetti boiling in a pot of water on the stove. He could see the silver strainer Mommy used to drain spaghetti nestled in the sink. Countless times, Peter watched Mommy turn off the stove, slip on her red oven mitts, carefully lift the heavy pot of spaghetti and water off the stove, carry it to the sink, and empty the big pot into the silver strainer that rested in the sink.

Countless times, Peter watched Mommy put the big pot on the counter and then lift the silver strainer out of the sink. Steam would rise as Peter watched the water drain through the holes in the strainer, and his mouth watered because he knew the best part was left behind – yummy spaghetti!

What does making spaghetti have to do with flowing thoughts?

Peter imagined his scary thoughts were like the water running through the little holes in the silver strainer. Peter imagined his happy thoughts were the delicious spaghetti left inside the silver strainer.

What were Peter's happy thoughts that he held in the silver strainer?

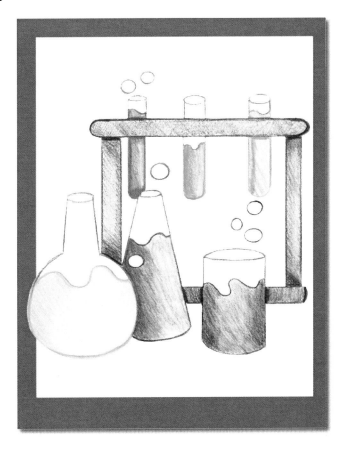

Peter thought about playing ''air drums'' with his Daddy when they listened to music. Peter thought about the snap of the rubber gloves he put on before he prepared his famous salad for customers at Cranberry Kitchens Family Restaurant. Peter thought about his sister Molly laughing and his Mommy clapping as they watched Peter sing and dance to a song he wrote. Peter thought about making concoctions with his scientist kit at home. Peter thought about many, many happy things. From the corner of his head (which was now filled with happy thoughts), he heard Daddy laughing. "Peter, what are you grinning about?" Daddy asked.

Peter's eyes popped open. He said, "I am thinking about my happy thoughts!" Peter looked around and saw the doctor wasn't in the room anymore. He squeezed his eyebrows together in confusion. "Daddy, when is the doctor going to check my blood?"

Daddy smiled at Peter and proudly announced, "The doctor finished! You were thinking happy thoughts and didn't even notice! You are a very brave and very smart little boy!"

Peter beamed. His flowing thoughts trick worked!

Peter was getting very sleepy, and before he knew it, he was deep in his dreams. Peter's dreams were happy because his head was filled with happy thoughts.

CHAPTER 5:

A FAMILY TALK

The next morning when Peter woke up, he looked around. He was still in the hospital. Mommy and Daddy were sitting in chairs next to Peter's bed. His little sister Molly was asleep in her stroller. She clenched her favorite stuffed animal, a fuzzy brown dog with floppy ears.

"What's going on?" asked Peter as he rubbed the sleep from his eyes. Mommy leaned over, to give Peter a kiss on his forehead and fix his hair. Peter smiled. Seeing his Mommy filled his heart with love.

Mommy squeezed Peter's hand and said, "Peter, your blood told the doctor a very important story. Your blood said that there is too much glucose (**gloo**-kose) in it. Glucose is a type of sugar that everyone's body needs. It gives your body energy to do fun things like swimming, running, and playing. But, too much glucose can make a body sick. Not enough glucose can also make a body sick."

Peter asked, "Is glucose like the story of Goldilocks? It can't be too much or too little, and it has to be just the right amount?"

Mommy and Daddy laughed. "Yes, Peter," Daddy said, "you have to have the right amount of glucose - not too much and not too little."

Peter nodded and said, "Glucose." Peter never heard that word before.

Peter squeezed his eyebrows in confusion. "How do I make sure I have the right amount of glucose in my body?"

Daddy held Peter's other hand and explained, "Do you remember how you make special concoctions at home with your scientist kit?"

Peter nodded.

"Well, there is a special concoction that helps to make sure that a body doesn't have too much or too little glucose. It's called insulin (**in**-suh-lin)."

Peter nodded and repeated, "Insulin." He never heard of this word either.

"Yes," Daddy continued. "Some people's bodies make insulin, and that insulin makes sure the amount of glucose in the body is just right. But, some people's bodies don't make insulin, so they need a special concoction to help them. Without it, there is too much glucose in their blood."

Peter nodded.

Mommy squeezed Peter's hand and said, "When a person's body needs the special insulin concoction, it's called diabetes (dye-uh-**be**-tees)."

Peter nodded and said, "Diabetes." Peter never heard that word either. He sure was learning a lot of new things!

"Yes," Mommy said, "Diabetes means that there is too much glucose in a person's body, and the special concoction of insulin helps that person's body feel better."

"Do I need the special concoction?" Peter asked.

Both Mommy and Daddy nodded their heads.

"Yes," said Mommy.

"You do," said Daddy.

CHAPTER 6:

A SPECIAL CONCOCTION

Daddy picked up a little device and showed it to Peter. "This is a blood glucose reader. We will use it on your finger to see if there is too much or too little glucose in your blood." Daddy handed the reader to Peter.

"How does it work," asked Peter as he turned it over in his hand and gave it back to Daddy.

"There are three steps," Daddy explained. "I'll show you on my finger."

"Step one," Daddy said as he held up little packet that said "alcohol" on it. He opened the packet and pulled out a little wet towel that looked just like the one Nurse Scott used the day before to clean Peter's arm. "We always clean our finger with the alcohol." Daddy demonstrated by wiping the little towel across the pad of his pointer finger.

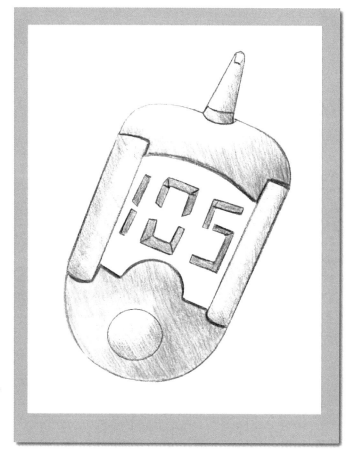

"Step two," Daddy said. He picked out a little plastic device. "This is a lancet (**lan**-set)." Daddy held the tip of lancet on his finger tip. Peter heard a faint click. Daddy set the lancet aside. A tiny drop of blood appeared on his finger.

"Step three," Mommy said. "We use a test strip and the reader to check our blood." She held the reader in one hand and took a small rectangular piece of paper from a container. She slipped it into the end of the reader, and part of the paper was sticking out.

"It looks like a frog with its tongue out!" exclaimed Peter

with a giggle.

"It sure does," agreed Mommy. She stuck her tongue out and made a frog face, which made Daddy and Peter burst into giggles.

Mommy reached out to grasp Daddy's hand, the hand where he held out his finger with the tiny drop of blood in the center of his fingertip. Mommy laid the paper on top of the blood, and Peter watched the screen on the reader. The number 80 appeared.

"The number 80 is a measure of how much sugar is in my blood," Daddy said.

"That's it," said Mommy with a big smile. She handed Daddy a little cotton ball, which he held on his fingertip. Mommy threw out the little piece of paper in a red trash can in the hospital room. Daddy pressed the cotton to his fingertip and then placed it in the red trash can.

"What's that?" Peter asked pointed to a little glass container on the counter. Mommy picked up the container and showed it to Peter.

Mommy replied, "This is a special insulin concoction. Your body needs it to make sure you don't have too much glucose in your blood. Daddy or I will use a tiny needle to help get the insulin inside your body."

Peter squeezed his eyebrows together. "Will it hurt?" he whispered.

"It will feel like a little pinch for just a moment," Daddy replied.

Peter frowned and whispered, "But I don't want to feel even a little pinch."

Mommy patted Peter's hand and agreed, "I know, Peter. It's okay to feel sad, but it's important to know that your body has the right amount of glucose."

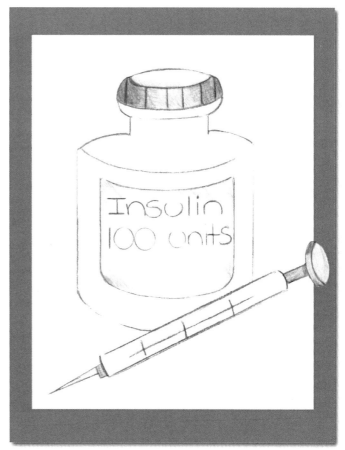

"We promise," added Daddy, "that you are going to feel so much better once you have the right amount of glucose in your body."

Peter thought to himself, 'Mommy and Daddy are right. I haven't been feeling so great.'

"And," Daddy continued, "to keep your body healthy, it's very important that we check your glucose regularly."

Peter frowned. He wanted to feel better, but he didn't want to get needles.

"After we check your glucose levels and make sure you have the right amount of insulin," Daddy added with a smile, "you can play on the very special drum set we have at home."

"Really?!" Peter squealed. He did NOT like the idea of getting a needle, but he DID LIKE the idea of playing on the drum set. Peter's Daddy was a drummer, and Peter couldn't wait to be big enough to play in a band with Daddy.

"Can you teach me how to play?" Peter asked. Peter loved listening to music with Daddy and playing "air drums." Now he would learn to play for real!

Mommy and Daddy laughed a BIG laugh. "Yes, yes, Peter," replied Daddy.

Mommy smiled at Daddy and then at Peter. She loved the idea of listening to the drums all day long!

Suddenly, an idea popped into Peter's head the way a light bulb appears in cartoons.

The idea was a brilliant idea.

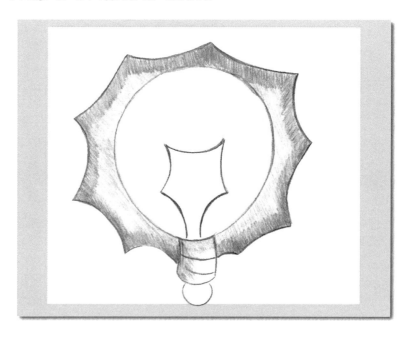

CHAPTER 7:

A BRILLIANT IDEA

Peter had a special talent for making up songs and dances. He could make up a song about anything and create a dance to go along with it. Many times, he made up songs and dances for his little sister Molly to make her smile and laugh while she got her diaper changed. Some of his best songs were about making concoctions with his science kit, making salads to sell at Cranberry Kitchens Family Restaurant, and, of course, about how delicious spaghetti is.

Peter's idea was to make up a song and dance that held happy thoughts in his head.

Peter took a deep breath. His eyes met Daddy's, and, in his bravest voice, he announced, "Okay. Let's do it."

Peter squeezed his eyes shut. He stuck out his pointer finger and wiggled it back and forth like a fish tail. The song bloomed in Peter's head and flowed from his lips.

Little red blood cells,

swimming all about.

What is going on with them?

*Let's find **out**!*

When Peter said "**out**," he held his pointer finger out to Daddy who cradled Peter's little hand in his big hand. He felt the tingle of the alcohol as Daddy wiped the pad of Peter's finger.

Little red blood cells,

swimming all about.

What can they tell us?

One pops **out**!

When Peter said "**out**," he heard the click of the lancet and felt a tiny pinch on his fingertip.

Little red blood cells,

singing us a song.

What are they saying?

"You are **strong**!"

When Peter said "**strong**," he felt the test paper being laid on top of his fingertip. It felt like a feather.

"Peter," Mommy laughed, "I love that song!" Peter's eyes opened in surprise. Could it be that his special song had magical powers? He wasn't scared at all!

"Now," Mommy continued, "we will give your body the insulin. Do you want to sing your song again?"

"Hmmmm," Peter said with a big smile and a twinkle in his eye. "I think I know what to do."

CHAPTER 8:

YOU ARE STRONG!

Peter lifted the sleeve of his tee-shirt so Mommy could give him the tiny needle in his arm. Peter closed his eyes. He imagined Mommy lifting the silver strainer in the sink.

All the scary thoughts flowed out of his mind as he imagined the water draining through the strainer. He thought about all the spaghetti left behind and all the wonderful things in his life. His head filled with happy thoughts.

Some of his happy thoughts were...

o Playing at the beach this past summer: Peter could smell the salty ocean air and taste the sweet lemonade from the boardwalk stand. He could feel the grains of sand in his hands as he sculpted castles. He could see the bright blue ocean stretch for miles before his eyes.

o Making concoctions with his science kit: Peter loved inspecting all the glass beakers filled with cool water and drops of brightly colored food dye. He could feel his wrist moving in circles as he watched the drops of color swirl and fill the entire container with one solid color. Peter could feel himself thinking about which containers to mix together to make new colors. His favorite was mixing the deep blue and bright yellow together to make the most glorious shade of green. Peter could see himself deciding and mixing and observing the changes.

○ Making his famous salad at Cranberry Kitchens Family Restaurant: Peter could feel the snap of the rubber gloves he put on when he prepared to make the salad. He could hear the crunch of the lettuce as he tore leaves to bite-size pieces. He could see the colorful fruit bowl where he would select between strawberries, blueberries, sliced apples, chopped pears, or apple chunks to add to his salad. Not many people think to add fruit to their salad. Peter knew that adding fruit is what made his salad so delicious and famous.

o Meeting his new baby sister Molly, when he officially became a big brother! Peter knew he wanted to and needed to stay strong and healthy so he could teach Molly many things, including the recipe for his famous special salad.

Peter sang:

Little red blood cells,

singing us a song.

What are they saying?

You are **<u>strong</u>**!

Little red blood cells,

racing all around.

How much glucose is there?

Just the right **<u>amount</u>**!

Peter opened his eyes to find Mommy and Daddy clapping and smiling. Molly had woken up and was clapping, too! Peter smiled back. He knew that making sure his body has the right amount of glucose wasn't going to be as much fun as a birthday party. However, Peter also knew that he wanted to feel better, feel strong and get back to work at Cranberry Kitchens Family Restaurant.

PETER'S SPECIAL SALAD

Ingredients:

lettuce

tomatoes

cucumbers

radishes

carrot slices

celery

(You can add any other veggies you like!)

Special Ingredients:

Add any of your favorite fruits!

Peter recommends: apple chunks, slices of pear, strawberries, blueberries, or watermelon.

Toppings you can add:

1. a sprinkle of cheese (Peter recommends parmesan.)
2. chopped nuts, but only if you aren't allergic (Peter recommends walnuts or almonds.)
3. croutons, which you can purchase and comes in different flavors.
4. craisins or raisins
5. crumbled tortilla chips

Directions:

1. Wash your hands. Wear gloves if you are preparing a salad to sell to others.
2. Have an adult wash and cut up all of the ingredients to bite size pieces.
3. You can tear up lettuce leaves or spinach leaves with your own hands.
4. Mixed everything together in a large bowl.
5. Add any salad dressing you like. Peter recommends a simple olive oil and vinegar mix.

"LITTLE RED BLOOD CELLS"

Little red blood cells,
swimming all about.
What is going on with them?
Let's find out!

Little red blood cells,
swimming all about.
What can they tell us?
 One pops **out**!

Little red blood cells,
singing us a song.
What are they saying?
"You are strong!"

Little red blood cells,
racing all around.
 How much glucose is there?
Just the right amount!

YOUR HAPPY THOUGHTS

Use this page to draw pictures of your happy thoughts.

DISCUSSION QUESTIONS

1. Is Type 1 Diabetes contagious (meaning others can catch it, like a cold)?

2. Can Type 1 Diabetes be prevented?

3. How do you feel when your blood sugar is too low?

4. How do you feel when your blood sugar is too high?

5. What are some worries you may have about having Type 1 Diabetes?

6. What are some interesting things you learned about Type 1 Diabetes?

7. Who can you talk to at school about having Type 1 Diabetes?

8. Who can you talk to at home about having Type 1 Diabetes?

WORD SEARCH

```
F H O S P I T A L T H T I I I
R L N I L U S N I Y Q C N B B
C A O G E Y D D A D L J A A V
U Z U W D N Q M R N E L S E R
F R V R I Y O E O C D T O O B
R X V A P N T E T M R M T M D
I S G G M E G I P A M C E E R
A U U U P R O T I Y O Y S S Q
I K X S U N H N H D T A R O T
R O E D S P E P S O G R U C J
D P I O O R P B L W U F N U T
R Z Q O W D A L A S Y G D L I
U Q P L D I A B E T E S H G M
M O L B S C I E N T I S T T U
S N C I T T E H G A P S H F S
```

AIR DRUMS	DOCTOR	INSULIN	SALAD
BEACH	FLOWING THOUGHTS	MOLLY	SCIENTIST
BLOOD SUGAR	GLUCOSE	MOMMY	SPAGHETTI
DADDY	HOSPITAL	NURSE	STRAINER
DIABETES	INJECTION	PETER	TYPE ONE

ABOUT THE AUTHOR

With 15 years of experience as a professional school counselor, Angela Cleveland has enjoyed working with a diverse population of students. Angela is a contributor to national publications, such as Edutopia, CSTA Voice, and ASCA's School Counselor magazine.

Angela's advocacy has earned her professional recognition, such as the NJ "2017 NJ State School Counselor of the Year."

Angela co-founded ReigningIt (www.ReigningIt.com), "creating a #STEM dialogue inclusive of every woman."

Learn more about Angela. Follow her on Twitter (@AngCleveland) and visit: www.AngelaCleveland.com.

ABOUT THE ILLUSTRATOR

Beth Pierce is an office worker by day, freelance cartoonist by night. She lives in New Jersey with her husband, daughter and two crazy cats.

Beth's artwork can be found on Instagram (instagram.com/littlebchan) and Tumblr (littlebchan.tumblr.com).

Made in United States
North Haven, CT
04 March 2022

16765506R00040